W9-CDK-314

My q Sound Box

by Jane Belk Moncure
illustrated by Linda Sommers

THE CHILD'S WORLD

MANKATO, MN 56001

Library of Congress Cataloging in Publication Data

Moncure, Jane Belk.
  M q sound box.

  (Sound box books)
  SUMMARY: A little girl fills her sound box
with many words beginning with the letter "q."
  [1. Alphabet] I. Sommers, Linda. II. Title.
III. Series.
PZ7.M739Myq   [E]   79-13085
ISBN 0-89565-100-9 -1991 Edition

My "q" Sound Box

(The letter "q" can be formed several different ways. The type-
face used throughout this book uses one form. Another form is
used on the front of the little moppet. These are two of the forms
that are commonly used today.)

Little  had a box.

"I will find things that begin with my 'q' sound," she said.

"I will put them into my sound  box."

Little q found quilts...

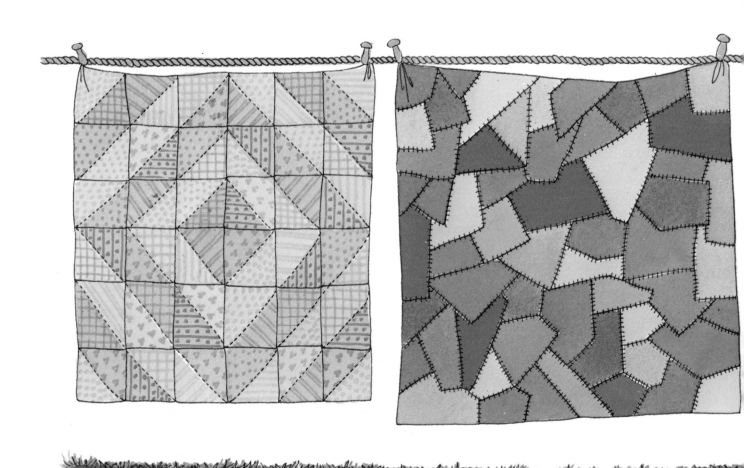

quite a lot of quilts.

Little q folded the quilts,

and filled her box with quilts.

box

There was one quilt left.

Little  wrapped the quilt around herself.

"I can be a queen," she said.

Just then, Little

met a real queen.

"If you want to look like a real queen,
you must have a crown," said the queen.

So Little  found some quarters...

quite a lot of quarters.

She counted her quarters.
How many did she have?

Little q took the

quarters to the store.

Little  q bought a crown.

The two queens played until they were hungry.

Little  q found a quart of milk

and a quart of quince jam.

Then she and the queen ate lunch.

Little q put what was

left into the box.

19

Then Little  said, "It's late! Let's go to bed."

"No! No!" said the queen. "A real queen must have a queen's bed."

Bed for a queen

Little  looked for more quarters

so that she could buy a queen's bed. She looked and looked. But she could not find any more quarters.

Then Little  saw her box with all the quilts inside.

"I will turn my box into a queen's bed," she said.

Little 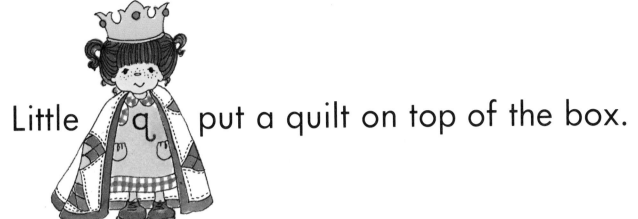 put a quilt on top of the box.

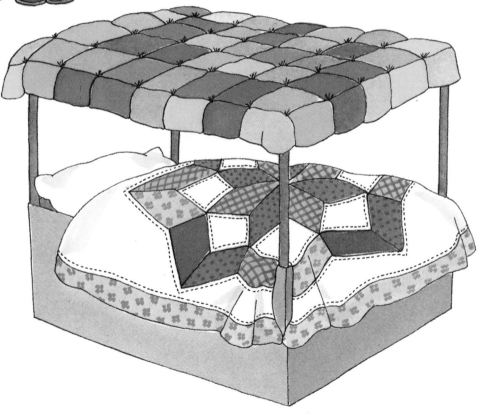

"Now let's go to bed," she said. She jumped into the box.

"No! No! No!" said the real queen.

So they quarreled and quarreled,

until  quarter past nine.

Then the real queen
was so tired of
quarreling that she quit!  And she

jumped into the box with Little
They pulled up the quilts
and went to sleep.

Can you read these words with Little ?

quartet

question mark

" quotation marks "

quiz

$\begin{array}{ccccc} 1 \\ +1 \end{array}$ $\begin{array}{c} 1 \\ +2 \end{array}$ $\begin{array}{c} 2 \\ +2 \end{array}$ $\begin{array}{c} 2 \\ +3 \end{array}$ $\begin{array}{c} 3 \\ +3 \end{array}$

$\begin{array}{c} 4 \\ -3 \end{array}$ $\begin{array}{c} 5 \\ -2 \end{array}$ $\begin{array}{c} 6 \\ -4 \end{array}$ $\begin{array}{c} 6 \\ -5 \end{array}$ $\begin{array}{c} 3 \\ -2 \end{array}$

$\begin{array}{c} 1 \\ \times 2 \end{array}$ $\begin{array}{c} 2 \\ \times 2 \end{array}$ $\begin{array}{c} 2 \\ \times 3 \end{array}$ $\begin{array}{c} 3 \\ \times 3 \end{array}$ $\begin{array}{c} 3 \\ \times 4 \end{array}$

$\begin{array}{c} 2 \\ \div 1 \end{array}$ $\begin{array}{c} 6 \\ \div 2 \end{array}$ $\begin{array}{c} 4 \\ \div 2 \end{array}$ $\begin{array}{c} 6 \\ \div 3 \end{array}$ $\begin{array}{c} 8 \\ \div 2 \end{array}$

quills

quail

quaker

quintuplets

quince

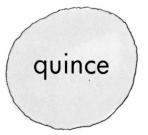

About the Author

Jane Belk Moncure, author of many books and stories for young children, is a graduate of Virginia Commonwealth University and Columbia University. She has taught nursery, kindergarten and primary children in Europe and America. Mrs. Moncure has taught early childhood education while serving on the faculties of Virginia Commonwealth University and the University of Richmond. She was the first president of the Virginia Association for Early Childhood Education and has been recognized widely for her services to young children. She is married to Dr. James A. Moncure, Vice President of Elon College, and currently teaches in Burlington, North Carolina.